alef-bet

Hi. My name is Gabi. This is a book about me, my brothers Uri and Lev, and my *ema* and *abba*. *Ema* and *abba* are the Hebrew words for mom and dad. My whole family speaks Hebrew. Now that I'm five, I can recite the alphabet, from *alef* to *tav*.

Can you find the letters as you look through this book? I'm teaching Lev. He knows *alef, bet* and *gimmel*.

Some sounds in Hebrew are funny, like *het*. My cousin Flory in America says it's like the sound you make when you gargle. My cousin Jonah says the *shin* sounds like "shh," what his mom says when his brother Micah is sleeping. And their friend Molly thinks the "tz" in *tzadeek* is the sound mosquitoes make when they buzz near her ear. You can think of things like this to help you remember the sound of Hebrew letters, too!

My mom writes children's books. But this is my book, and since I don't know how to write yet, I'm telling my story in pictures. Every page tells a story, so there's a lot to talk about and look for on each one. Can you find the *ambatya*, the bathtub? That's where I get to play with water. Sometimes I let Lev join me: he makes great waves! How many rubber ducks can you find on that page? My brother Uri loves fish; sometimes he lets me feed his fish in the tank in our kitchen.

Uri and I both like to draw and make crafts. Lucky for us, our dad owns an art supply store. If you like, you can follow me through my book and see some of my art. What do you like to draw and paint?

My brothers don't like playing Getting Married much or pretending to be a cat, but we all love sledding and pillow fights. Our whole family likes nature, watching the moon, and even raking leaves. What things do you like to do with your family?

Now that you know a bit about us, you can make up your own stories about the pictures in my book. You can look at this book over and over again, and see and learn something different each time you open it. Try and sound out the words. Maybe, someday, you'll greet me by saying *Shalom*.

alef-bet

In memory of
Florence and Milton Gessner

Thanks to Sandy Brawarsky, Henriette Goldstein, James Gordon, Marcia Kaunfer, Rabbi Daniel Levine, Dr. Joseph Lowin, and Ayal Vogul for their help with the Hebrew material, and to Natalie Blitt for all your support and encouragement.

A SPECIAL THANK YOU TO FAYE R. HOUSE, PHYSICAL THERAPIST, for her help, support, and criticism in the creation and drawing of Uri (see author's note). Any mistakes or oversights are mine.

Junebug Books, 105 South Court Street, Montgomery, AL 36104. Copyright © 2008 by Michelle Edwards. All rights reserved under International and Pan-American Copyright Conventions. Published in the United States by Junebug Books, a division of NewSouth, Inc., Montgomery, Alabama.

Library of Congress Cataloging-in-Publication Data

Edwards, Michelle.
Alef-bet : a Hebrew alphabet book / by Michelle Edwards.
p. cm.
Originally published: New York : Lothrop, Lee & Shepard Books, c1992.
ISBN-13: 978-1-58838-233-7 • ISBN-10: 1-58838-233-8
1. Hebrew language—Alphabet—Juvenile literature. I. Title.
PJ4589.E38 2008
492.4'813—dc22

2008043346

Printed and bound in Singapore by Tien Wah Press Pte Ltd.

alef-bet

A HEBREW ALPHABET BOOK

by michelle edwards

Junebug Books

Montgomery | Louisville

א

alef

אַמְבַּטְיָה

(ahm-BAHT-yah)

bathtub

בּ

bet

בָּרָק

(bah-RAHK)

lightning

גּ

gimel

גַּרְבַּיִם

(gar-BAH-yim)

socks

ד

dalet

דָּגִים

(dah-GEEM)

fish

ה

hay

הוֹרִים

(hoh-REEM)   parents

ו
vav

וֶרֶד
(VEH-red)

rose

ז

zayin

זָקָן

(zah-KAHN)

beard

ח

het

חָתוּל
(chah-TOOL)

cat

tet

(tee-pah)

drop

yod

(yahd)

hand

kaf

כּוֹבַע

(KOH-vah)

hat

לamed

lamed

לְבָנָה

(leh-vah-NAH)

moon

מ

mem

מִפְלֶצֶת

(meh-FLEHT-zeht)

monster

נ
nun

נוֹצוֹת
(noh-TZOHT)

feathers

ס

samekh

סְתָו

(stahv)

autumn

ayin

עָנָק
(ah-NAHK)

giant

pay

פַּרְפָּרִים
(pahr-pah-REEM)   butterflies

tzadeek

צַעֲצוּעִים

(tzah-tzoo-EEM)

toys

ק

kof

קוֹפִים

(koh-FEEM)

monkeys

ר

resh

רַגְלַיִם

(rah-GLAH-yeem)

feet

shin

(SHEH-legg)

snow

ת

tav

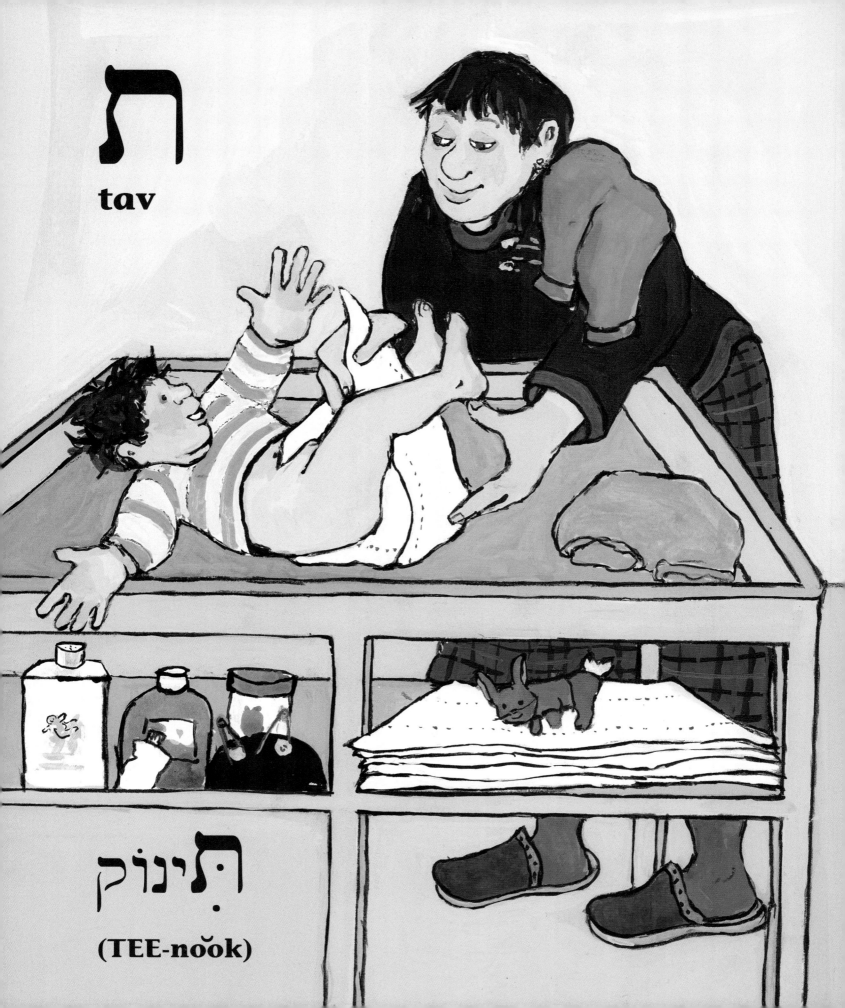

תִּינוֹק

(TEE-noŏk)

baby

A Note from the Author

The family in this book speaks Hebrew. They may know other languages as well, such as English, French, or Spanish. They may live in Jerusalem, New York, or Amsterdam. There are Hebrew speakers in almost every corner of the world: it's not just Israelis who speak the language in their homes and with their friends and family.

Although they are fictional, the characters in this book have become my friends. Hannah is the *ema*, the mom. Matan is the *abba*, the dad. Uri (age 9) is the oldest child; then comes Gabi (age 5); and little Lev, the toddler (almost 2).

Like me, Hannah is a children's book writer, and Matan owns an art-supply store. Uri goes to school and is quite a good artist. He uses a wheelchair because he was born with spina bifida and is unable to move his legs. Gabi likes polka dots, dancing, make-believe, dressing up, and goofing around with Uri when he lets her. Lev likes his tire sandbox, stroller rides, kicking his feet at the moon, and goofing around with Uri and Gabi when they let him.

Hannah, Matan, Uri, and Gabi all came to life during wartime, so Gabi ends her book with *shalom*, the Hebrew word for hello, goodbye, and peace. It is her wish and mine that you may read this book in peace.

Using This Book With Young Listeners

While reading this book, some children may enjoy hearing the sounds of the Hebrew letters and words, while others will prefer to focus on the book's joyous illustrations. Here are examples of questions you might ask as you and your child are exploring *Alef-Bet*. We hope you enjoy getting to know Gabi and her very special family.

Questions to ask as you read:

Look at Uri's fish tank and see if you can find the yellow and black clown fish. These are Gabi's favorites. Which *dah-GEEM* (fish) do you like best? How many deep-sea divers can you find in the tank?

Sometimes Gabi pretends to be a mommy. Can you find the page where she is taking care of the *koh-FEEM* (monkeys)? Uh-oh! It looks like one baby monkey has lost something. What is he missing?

Gabi loves to draw and make crafts. Can you find the page where she has made lots and lots of handprints? Can you find the blue *yahd* (hand)? What color did Gabi paint the fingernails?

Have fun with the pictures in this book! Try making questions and stories of your own! *Shalom*!

How to Use this Book

Each letter of the Hebrew alphabet appears in the upper left corner of each page or two-page spread in this book. Its transliteration into Roman letters appears beneath it. The Hebrew words appear on the lower left with their pronunciations beneath them, and their English translations in the lower right-hand corner of the page.

Hebrew is read from right to left; the marks beneath or within some of the letters in a word are vowels. Hebrew is often written without vowels, but they have been included here for beginning readers. There are no capital letters in Hebrew; the first letter of each Hebrew word in the book appears larger for the purpose of easy identification.

There are some sounds in Hebrew that have no English equivalents. To help connect the Hebrew letters with their sounds, the list below gives the closest approximations. And just as there are accents and dialects in all languages, so too may some Hebrew speakers pronounce the letters and words in this book somewhat differently.

א	ALEF	takes the sound of its accompanying vowel	ל	LAMED	L as in Like
ב	BET	B as in Boy	מ	MEM	M as in Mouse
ג	GIMEL	G as in Goat	נ	NUN	N as in Nice
ד	DALET	D as in Dog	ס	SAMEKH	S as in Sun
ה	HAY	H as in Happy	ע	AYIN	takes the sound of its accompanying vowel
ו	VAV	V as in Voice	פ	PAY	P as in Papa
ז	ZAYIN	Z as in Zoo	צ	TZADEEK	TZ as in TZar
ח	HET	CH as in Challah	ק	KOF	K as in Kangaroo
ט	TET	T as in Toy	ר	RESH	R as in Run
י	YOD	Y as in Yo-yo	ש	SHIN	SH as in SHip
כ	KAF	K as in Kangaroo	ת	TAV	T as in Toy